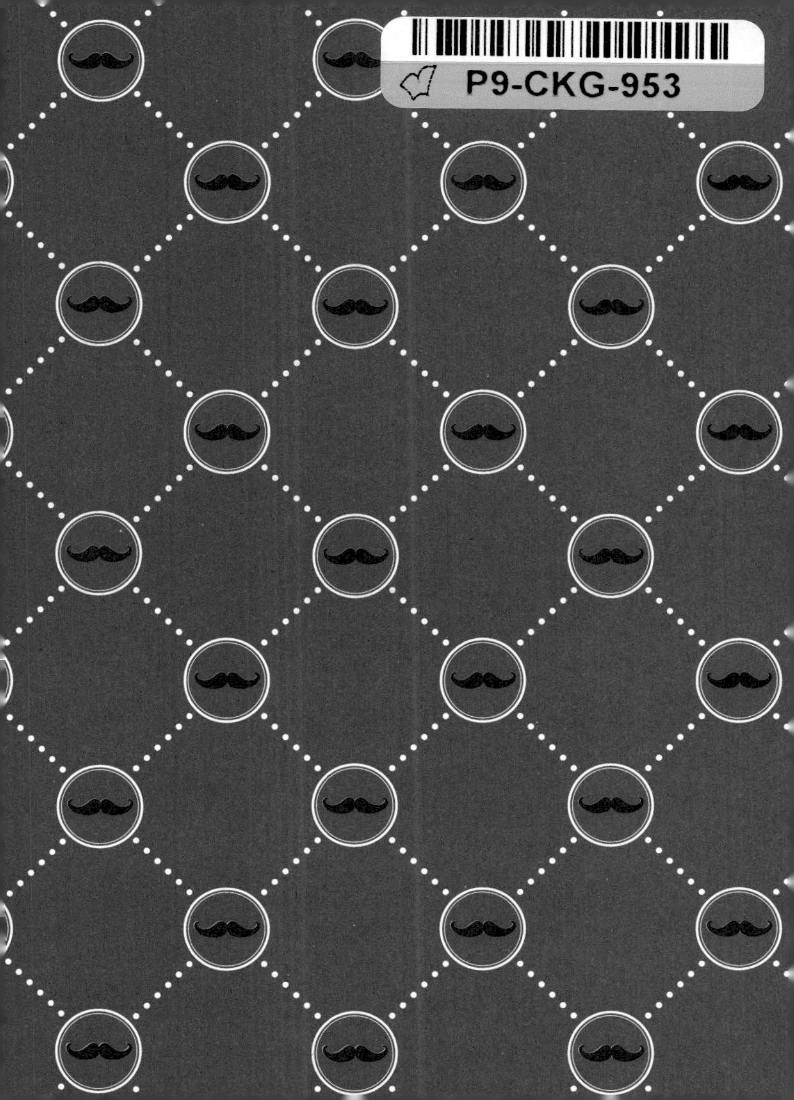
P9-CKG-953

LITTLE GREY CELLS

'In the little grey cells of the brain lies the solution of every mystery.'

'The King of Clubs'

— THE HERCULE POIROT BOOKS —

The Mysterious Affair at Styles
The Murder on the Links
Poirot Investigates
The Murder of Roger Ackroyd
The Big Four
The Mystery of the Blue Train
Peril at End House
Lord Edgware Dies
Murder on the Orient Express
Three Act Tragedy
Death in the Clouds
The ABC Murders
Murder in Mesopotamia
Cards on the Table
Murder in the Mews
Dumb Witness
Death on the Nile
Appointment With Death
Hercule Poirot's Christmas
Sad Cypress
One, Two, Buckle My Shoe
Evil Under the Sun
Five Little Pigs
The Hollow
The Labours of Hercules
Taken at the Flood
Mrs McGinty's Dead
After the Funeral
Hickory Dickory Dock
Dead Man's Folly
Cat Among the Pigeons
The Adventure of the Christmas Pudding
The Clocks
Third Girl
Hallowe'en Party
Elephants Can Remember
Poirot's Early Cases
Curtain: Poirot's Last Case

— POIROT ALSO FEATURES IN —

Problem at Pollensa Bay
While the Light Lasts
Hercule Poirot and the Greenshore Folly
Black Coffee *novelised by Charles Osborne*
The Monogram Murders *by Sophie Hannah*

Agatha Christie®

LITTLE GREY CELLS

The Quotable POIROT

Edited by David Brawn

wm
WILLIAM MORROW
An Imprint of HarperCollins*Publishers*

This is a work of fiction. Names, characters, places, and incidents are products of the author's imagination or are used fictitiously and are not to be construed as real. Any resemblance to actual events, locales, organizations, or persons, living or dead, is entirely coincidental.

HarperCollins books may be purchased for educational, business, or sales promotional use. For information, please email the Special Markets Department at SPsales@harpercollins.com.

Originally published in the UK in 2015 by HarperCollins UK.

FIRST WILLIAM MORROW EDITION

Library of Congress Cataloging-in-Publication Data has been applied for.

ISBN 978-0-06-242517-1

16 17 18 19 20 SCP 10 9 8 7 6 5 4 3 2 1

CONTENTS

INTRODUCTION

LIVING WITH POIROT

by Agatha Christie

'Poirot was an extraordinary-looking little man. He was hardly more than five feet four inches, but carried himself with great dignity. His head was exactly the shape of an egg, and he always perched it a little on one side. His moustache was very stiff and military. The neatness of his attire was almost incredible; I believe a speck of dust would have caused him more pain than a bullet wound. Yet this quaint dandified little man who, I was sorry to see, now limped badly, had been in his time one of the most celebrated members of the Belgian police. As a detective, his flair had been extraordinary, and he had achieved triumphs by unravelling some of the most baffling cases of the day.'

The Mysterious Affair at Styles

How did the character of Hercule Poirot come into being?

Difficult to say – and I realise that he made his appearance not at all in the manner he himself would have wished! 'Hercule Poirot first,' he would have said, 'and *then* a plot to display his remarkable talents to the best advantage.' But it was not so. The plot of the story, *The Mysterious Affair at Styles*, was roughed out, and then came the dilemma: a detective story – now what kind of detective?

It was in the early autumn of 1914 – Belgian refugees were in most country places. Why not have a Belgian refugee, a former shining light of the Belgian Police force?

What kind of a man should he be? A little man, perhaps, with a somewhat grandiloquent name. Hercule something? Hercule Poirot? Yes, that would do. He should be very neat – very orderly. (Is that because I am a wildly untidy person myself?)

Such was the first rough outline – mostly, you will note, externals – but certain traits followed almost automatically. Like many small dandified men, he would be conceited and he would of course (why, of course!) have a handsome moustache.

That was the beginning. Hercule Poirot emerged from the mists and took concrete shape and form. There was more in the little man than I had ever suspected. There was, for instance, his intense interest in the psychology of every case. As early as *The Murder on the Links* he was showing his appreciation of the mental processes of a murderer and insisting that every crime had a definite signature. Method and order still meant much to him.

And now, what of the relations between us – between the creator and the created? Well – let me confess it – there has been at times a coolness between us! There are moments when I have felt: 'Why–why–why did I ever invent this detestable, bombastic, tiresome little creature?'

Eternally straightening things, eternally boasting, eternally twirling his moustache and tilting his egg-shaped head. Anyway, what is an egg-shaped head? When people say to me, 'Which way *up* is the egg?' – do I really know? I don't, because I never do see pictorial things clearly, but nevertheless I know that he has an egg-shaped head covered with suspiciously black hair, and I know his eyes occasionally shine with a green light. Twice in my life I have actually seen him – once on a boat going to the Canary Islands, and once having lunch at the Savoy. I have said to myself: 'Now, if you had only had the nerve, you could have "snap-shotted" that man in the boat, and then when people have said, "Yes, but what is he like?" you could perhaps have produced that snap shot and explained matters.' But life is full of lost opportunities.

If you are doubly burdened, first by acute

shyness, and secondly by only seeing the right thing to do or say twenty-four hours later, what can you do? Only write about quick-witted men and resourceful girls, whose reactions are like greased lightning!

Yes, there have been moments when I have disliked M. Hercule Poirot very much indeed, when I have rebelled bitterly against being yoked to him for life. (Usually at one of these moments I receive a fan letter saying: 'I know you must love your little detective by the way you write about him.')

But now, I must confess it, Hercule Poirot has won. A reluctant affection has sprung up for him. He has become more human, less irritating. I admire certain things about him – his passion for the truth, his understanding of human frailty, and his kindliness. And he has taught me something – to take more interest in my own characters; to see them more as real people and less as pawns in a game.

In spite of his vanity he often chooses

deliberately to stand aside and let the main drama develop. He says, in effect, 'It is their story – let them show you why and how this happened.' He knows, all right, that the star part is going to be his later. He may make his appearance at the very end of the first act, but he will take the centre of the stage in the second act, and his big scene at the end of the third act is a mathematical certainty.

19 January 1938

'Words, mademoiselle, are only the outer clothing of ideas.'

The ABC Murders

1

‘JE SUIS . . .’

'My name is Hercule Poirot, and I am probably the greatest detective in the world.'

The Mystery of the Blue Train

'The false moustache! *Quelle Horreur!* Never, in the whole of London, have I seen a pair of moustaches to equal mine.'

The ABC Murders

'It is sometimes difficult for a dog to find a scent, but once he has found it, nothing on earth will make him leave it! That is if he is a good dog! And I, Hercule Poirot, am a very good dog.'

'The Chocolate Box'

'This street, it is not aristocratic, *mon ami*! In it there is no fashionable doctor, no fashionable dentist – still less is there a fashionable milliner! But there is a fashionable detective.'

'The Adventure of the Western Star'

'I am better than the police.'

The ABC Murders

'I am not mad. I am eccentric perhaps – at least certain people say so; but as regards my profession. I am very much as one says, "all there".'

The Mystery of the Blue Train

'I like an audience, I must confess.
I am vain, you see. I am puffed up with
conceit. I like to say, "See how clever is
Hercule Poirot!"'

Death on the Nile

'To the intelligence of Hercule Poirot the case is perfectly clear, but for the benefit of others, not so greatly gifted by the good God – it would be as well to make a few inquiries to establish the facts. One must have consideration for those less gifted than oneself.'

'The Million Dollar Bond Robbery'

'In my own particular line, there is no one to touch me. *C'est dommage!* As it is, I admit freely and without hypocrisy that I am a great man. I have the order, the method and the psychology in an unusual degree. I am, in fact, Hercule Poirot! Why should I turn red and stammer and mutter into my chin that really I am very stupid? It would not be true.'

'The Mystery of the Baghdad Chest'

'When one is unique, one knows it!'

'The Adventure of the Western Star'

'Je suis un peu snob.'

The Hollow

2

FOOD & DRINK

'If you are going into exile, a good cook may be of more comfort than a pretty face.'

'The Adventure of the Clapham Cook'

'The cooking, it is English at its worst. Those Brussels sprouts so enormous, so hard, that the English like so much. The potatoes boiled and either hard or falling to pieces. The vegetables that taste of water, water, and again water. The complete absence of the salt and pepper in any dish.'

Curtain

'Only in England is the coffee so atrocious. On the Continent they understand how important it is for the digestion that it should be properly made.'

The Big Four

'*Good* English cooking, not the cooking one gets in the second-class hotels or restaurants, is much appreciated by *gourmets* on the continent... They wrote, "It is worth making a journey to London just to taste the varieties and excellences of the English puddings." And above all puddings is the Christmas plum pudding.'

'The Adventure of the Christmas Pudding'

'The sherry, I prefer it to the cocktail, and a thousand times to the whisky. *Ah, quel horreur*, the whisky. But drinking the whisky, you ruin, absolutely ruin, the palate. The delicate wines of France, to appreciate them, you must never *never*...'

Three Act Tragedy

'Alas, that one can eat only three times a day... If one partakes of the five o'clock, one does not approach the dinner with the proper quality of expectant gastric juices. And the dinner, let us remember, is the supreme meal of the day!'

Mrs McGinty's Dead

'*Mon Dieu!* It is that in this country you treat the affairs gastronomic with a criminal indifference.'

'The Adventure of the Western Star'

3

HUMAN NATURE

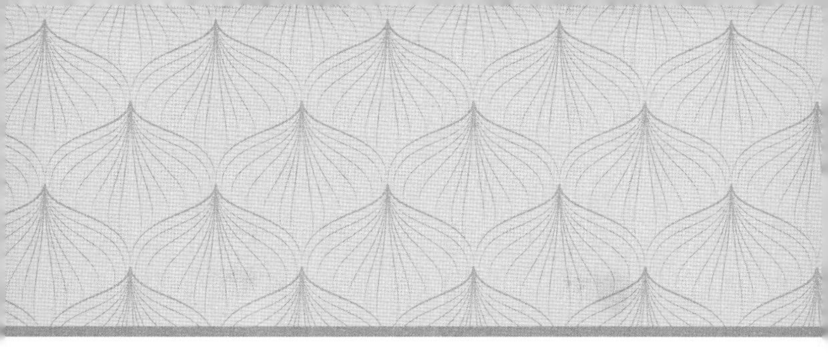

'Wherever there is human nature, there is drama. But – it is not always just where you think it is.'

'The King of Clubs'

'There is nothing so intangible, so difficult to pin down, as the source of a rumour.'

The Labours of Hercules

'The Lernean Hydra'

'A man may work towards a certain object, may labour and toil to attain a certain kind of leisure and occupation, and then find that, after all, he yearns for the old busy days, and the old occupations that he thought himself so glad to leave? The object gained, we find that what we miss is the daily toil.'

The Murder of Roger Ackroyd

‘Bad temper is its own safety valve.
He who can bark does not bite.’

‘The Under Dog’

'Every murderer is probably somebody's old friend. You cannot mix up sentiment and reason.'

The Mysterious Affair at Styles

'*Stupidity* – it is the sin that is never forgiven and always punished.'

Cards on the Table

‘Human curiosity. Such a very interesting thing… A little boy watches his mother’s kettle raising its lid because of the steam. And the next thing we know is we have railway trains, leading on in due course to railway strikes and all that.’

Elephants Can Remember

'It is useless to dispense energy by unnecessary action. There is a golden rule in life – never do anything yourself that others can do for you. Especially when expense is no object!'

The Labours of Hercules

'The Apples of the Hesperides'

‘Doubtless *le bon Dieu* knows what he does. But it is odd that he should have permitted himself to fashion certain human beings.’

‘The Triangle at Rhodes’

4

'LES FEMMES'

‘I have made it a rule never to argue with very positive ladies. You comprehend, it is a waste of time.’

‘The Under Dog’

'*Les femmes*... they are marvellous! They invent haphazard – and by miracle they are right. Not that it is that, really. Women observe subconsciously a thousand little details, without knowing that they are doing so. Their subconscious mind adds these little things together – and they call the result intuition'

The Murder of Roger Ackroyd

'To count – really and truly to count – a woman must have goodness or brains.'

Evil Under the Sun

‘The heart of a woman who loves will forgive many blows.’

The Murder on the Links

'*Les femmes* – whatever it is – they always want it *now*, do they not?'

The Labours of Hercules

'The Horses of the Diomedes'

'Knees are a very good indication of age. The knees of a woman of twenty-three or twenty-four can never really be mistaken for the knees of a girl of fourteen or fifteen.'

Cat Among the Pigeons

'Convention decrees that a woman must make a decent pretence of mourning for her husband.'

'The Tragedy at Marsdon Manor'

'*Why* does a woman keep a photograph of herself when young? She has been a pretty girl and she keeps a photograph of herself to remind her of what a pretty girl she was. It encourages her when her mirror tells her unpalatable things.'

Mrs McGinty's Dead

'Does not a young man notice when a girl is pretty? ... Me, I always notice when a girl is pretty.'

'The Incredible Theft'

‘Mothers are particularly ruthless when their children are in danger.’

Death on the Nile

'As an older man, a very much older man, I venture to offer you a piece of advice. A very wise friend of mine in the Police Force said to me years ago: "Hercule, my friend, if you would know tranquillity, avoid women."'

Evil Under the Sun

5

THE ENGLISH

‘Ah, *mais c’est anglais* ça, everything in black and white, everything clear cut and well defined. But life, it is not like that.’

The Mystery of the Blue Train

‘Though I am a foreigner, I know something of the English point of view. I know, for instance, that there are “things which are done” and “things which are not done”.’

Death on the Nile

'The English people, they have a mania for the fresh air. The big air, it is all very well outside, where it belongs. Why admit it to the house?'

The Murder of Roger Ackroyd

'It is true that I can speak the exact, the idiomatic English. But, my friend, to speak the broken English is an enormous asset. It leads people to despise you. They say – *a foreigner* – he can't even speak English properly... And so, you see, I put people off their guard. Besides – it has become a habit.'

Three Act Tragedy

‘I have made my little observations of your English nation, and a lady, a born lady, is always particular about her shoes. She may have shabby clothes, but she will be well shod.’

‘The Veiled Lady’

'He speaks too many languages for a good Englishman! (Pardon me, as linguists, you are deplorable!)'

'The Kidnapped Prime Minister'

'No one will observe us. The Sunday concert, the Sunday "afternoon out", and finally the Sunday nap after the Sunday dinner of England – *le rosbif* – all these will distract attention from the doings of Hercule Poirot.'

'The Adventure of the Cheap Flat'

6

SYMMETRY & ORDER

Twenty-four hours...

'And a quarter. Do not forget the quarter, monsieur – it may come in useful.'

'The Kidnapped Prime Minister'

‘The tallest books go in the top shelf, the next tallest in the row beneath, and so on. Thus we have order, *method*.’

‘The Adventure of the Western Star’

‘He interested me because he was trying to grow a moustache and as yet the result is poor. It is an art, the growing of the moustache! I have sympathy for all who attempt it.’

‘Double Sin’

‘It is really insupportable that every hen lays an egg of a different size! What symmetry can there be on the breakfast table?’

‘The Disappearance of Mr Davenheim’

'The Pyramids – they, at least, are of a shape solid and geometrical, but their surface is of an unevenness most unpleasing. And the palm-trees, I like them not. Not even do they plant them in rows.'

'The Adventure of the Egyptian Tomb'

'*Golf*... What a game! Figure to yourself, each hole it is of a different length. The obstacles, they are not arranged mathematically. Even the greens are frequently up one side! There is only one pleasing thing – the how do you call them? Tee boxes! They, at least, are symmetrical.'

The Murder on the Links

‘I always make my plans well in advance. To succeed in life every detail should be arranged well beforehand.’

Death on the Nile

'This piece of toast. Is it square? No. Is it a triangle? Again no. Is it even round? No. Is it of any shape remotely pleasing to the eye? What symmetry have we here? None. Comprehend you not that I have forbidden such a loaf – a loaf haphazard and shapeless, that no baker should permit himself to bake!'

The Murder on the Links

‘If you must wear a tie pin, Hastings, at least let it be in the exact centre of your tie. At present it is at least a sixteenth of an inch too much to the right.’

‘The Adventure of Johnny Waverly’

7

ROMANCE

'It is deplorable! To remove all the romance – all the mystery! Today everything is *standardized!*'

Evil Under the Sun

‘I am not, like the English, romantic. To arrange a good marriage, one must take more than *romance* into consideration.’

Dead Man’s Folly

'In the midst of death we are in life... Murder, I have often noticed, is a great matchmaker.'

The ABC Murders

'Jealousy, however far-fetched and extravagant it may seem, is nearly always based on *reality*. There is a saying, is there not, that the customer is always right? Well, the same is true of the jealous husband or wife. However little *concrete* evidence there may be, *fundamentally* they are always right.'

The Labours of Hercules

'The Lernean Hydra'

‘It is droll, the way they arrange
the marriages over here. No order.
No method. Everything left to chance.’

‘Christmas Adventure’

'Village gossip, it is based always, always on the relations of the sexes. If a man poisons his wife in order to travel to the North Pole or to enjoy the peace of a bachelor existence – it would not interest his fellow villagers for a minute! It is because they are convinced that the murder has been committed in order *that the man may marry another woman* that the talk grows and spreads.'

The Labours of Hercules

'The Lernean Hydra'

'What a wonderful dispensation it is of Nature's that every man, however superficially unattractive, should be some woman's choice.'

Mrs McGinty's Dead

'Often a nice respectable woman of that age leaves a husband she has lived with for twenty years, and sometimes a whole family of children as well, in order to link her life with that of a young man considerably her junior... In the autumn of a woman's life, there comes always one mad moment when she longs for romance, for adventure – before it is too late.'

'The Cornish Mystery'

'You have the good heart to think of an old man. And the good heart, it is in the end worth all the little grey cells.'

'The Jewel Robbery at the Grand Metropolitan'

8

LIFE AND DEATH

'Put your trust in God, and keep your powder dry.'

Dead Man's Folly

'Life is like that! It does not permit you to arrange and order it as you will. It will not permit you to escape emotion, to live by the intellect and by reason! You cannot say, "I will feel so much and no more." Life, whatever else it is, is not *reasonable*.'

Sad Cypress

‘He was not nice, no. But he was alive and now he is dead, and as I told him once, I have a *bourgeois* attitude to murder, I disapprove of it.’

Cards on the Table

'Death, mademoiselle, unfortunately creates a *prejudice* in favour of the deceased – "She was bright. She was happy. She was sweet-tempered. She had not a care in the world. She had no undesirable acquaintances." – There is a great charity always to the dead.'

The ABC Murders

‘The wages of sin are said to be death. But sometimes the wages of sin seem to be luxury. Is that any more endurable, I wonder?’

Taken at the Flood

'Not only is truth stranger than fiction – it is more dramatic.'

'The King of Clubs'

'Evil never goes unpunished. But the punishment is sometimes secret.'

Peril at End House

'The victim may be one of the good God's saints – or, on the contrary – a monster of infamy. It moves me not. The fact is the same. A life – taken! I say it always – I do not approve of murder.'

Appointment with Death

'There are things that cannot be hurried – *le bon Dieu*, Nature, and old people.'

The Mystery of the Blue Train

'Here's an Englishman mysteriously done to death in Holland. They always say that – and later they find that he ate the tinned fish and that his death is perfectly natural.'

'The Veiled Lady'

'Life is like a train, Mademoiselle. It goes on. And it is a good thing that that is so. Because the train gets to its journey's end at last, and there is a proverb about that in your language, Mademoiselle. "Journeys end in lovers meeting." Trust the train, Mademoiselle, for it is *le bon Dieu* who drives it. And trust Hercule Poirot. He knows.'

The Mystery of the Blue Train

9

DETECTIVE WORK

'Everything must be taken into account. If the fact will not fit the theory – let the theory go.'

The Mysterious Affair at Styles

'One of the advantages, or disadvantages, of being a detective is that it brings you into contact with the criminal classes. And they can teach you some very interesting and curious things.'

'Wasp's Nest'

'One does not employ merely the muscles. I do not need to bend and measure the footprints and pick up the cigarette ends and examine the bent blades of grass. It is enough for me to sit back in my chair and *think*.'

Five Little Pigs

'Imagination is a good servant, and a bad master. The simplest explanation is always the most likely.'

The Mysterious Affair at Styles

'Instinct is a marvellous thing. It can neither be explained nor ignored.'

The Mysterious Affair at Styles

‘It is always the facts that will not fit in that are significant.’

Death on the Nile

‘If you show the dog the rabbit, he goes into the rabbit hole. The dog hunts rabbits. Hercule Poirot hunts murderers... And I am going into the burrow after him.’

Dumb Witness

'There is nothing so dangerous *for anyone who has something to hide* as conversation! Speech, so a wise old Frenchman said to me once, is an invention of man's to prevent him from thinking. It is also an infallible means of discovering that which he wishes to hide. Every time he will give himself away.'

The ABC Murders

'I find it a good sign when a case is obscure. If a thing is clear as daylight – *eh bien*, mistrust it! Someone has made it so.'

'The Disappearance of Mr Davenheim'

‘If the little grey cells are not exercised, they grow the rust.’

The ABC Murders

‘The past is the father of the present.’

Hallowe’en Party

‘I mean to arrive at the truth. The truth, however ugly in itself, is always curious and beautiful to the seeker after it.’

The Murder of Roger Ackroyd

‘The impossible cannot have happened, therefore the impossible must be possible in spite of appearances.’

Murder on the Orient Express

10

THE CRIMINAL MIND

‘They fear me, Hastings; the criminals of your England they fear me! When the cat is there, the little mice, they come no more to the cheese!’

‘The Veiled Lady’

'You are wise.
Trust no one.'

'The Incredible Theft'

'I can admire the perfect murder – I can also admire a tiger – that splendid tawny-striped beast. But I will admire him from *outside* his cage. I will not go inside.'

Cards on the Table

'Have you ever said suddenly to anyone, "Throw a stone and see if you can hit that tree," and the person obeys quickly without thinking—and surprisingly often he *does* hit the tree. But when he comes to repeat the throw it is not so easy, for he has begun to *think*. There is a type of crime like that – a crime committed on the spur of the moment – an inspiration – a flash of genius – without time to pause or think.'

Cards on the Table

'It is the quietest and meekest people who are often capable of the most sudden and unexpected violence . . . when their control does snap, it goes entirely!'

Hercule Poirot's Christmas

‘There are things that my profession has taught me. And one of these things, the most terrible thing is this: *Murder is a habit.*’

Murder in Mesopotamia

'Man is an unoriginal animal. If a man commits a crime, any other crime he commits will resemble it closely... When you have two crimes precisely similar in design and execution, you find the same brain behind them both.'

The Murder on the Links

'If you care for money too much, it is only the money you see, everything else is in shadow.'

Lord Edgware Dies

'Once a man is imbued with the idea that he knows who ought to be allowed to live and who ought not – then he is half way to becoming the most dangerous killer there is.'

Cards on the Table

11

TRUTH & LIES

'I do not take sides. I am on the side only of the truth.'

One, Two, Buckle My Shoe

'You tell your lies and you think nobody knows. But there are two people who know. Yes – two people. One is *le bon Dieu*. And the other is Hercule Poirot.'

The Mystery of the Blue Train

'No, my friend, I am not drunk. It is that I have been to the dentist, and need not return for another six months. It is a beautiful thought.'

One, Two, Buckle My Shoe

'The newspapers, they are so inaccurate. I never go by what they say.'

Sad Cypress

‘*If* one is going to tell a lie at all, it might as well be an artistic lie, a romantic lie, a convincing lie.’

Dumb Witness

‘There appears to be no mouse in this mouse-hole… Still, life is full of discrepancies.’

‘The Tragedy at Marsdon Manor’

'The dog, he argues from reason. *Eh bien,* who is the person who most persistently tries to gain admission, rattling on the door twice or three times a day – and who is never by any chance admitted? The postman. Clearly, then, an undesirable guest – but he persistently returns and tries again. Then a dog's duty is clear, to aid in driving this undesirable man away, and to bite him if possible. A most reasonable proceeding.'

Dumb Witness

'A guess is either right or wrong. If it is right you call it an intuition. If it is wrong you usually do not speak of it again.'

The ABC Murders

'I believe in the terrific force of superstition. Get it firmly established that a series of deaths are supernatural, and you might almost stab a man in broad daylight, and it would still be put down to the curse, so strongly is the instinct of the supernatural implanted in the human race.'

'The Adventure of the Egyptian Tomb'

‘If you could not make the best of both worlds, you could not be a politician.’

‘The Incredible Theft’

'When you find that people are not telling you the truth – look out!'

The Mysterious Affair at Styles

12

‘MY DEAR HASTINGS’

'I reserve the explanations for the last chapter.'

Evil Under the Sun

'You know, Hastings, in many ways
I regard you as my mascot.'

The ABC Murders

'After reading the newspaper, I folded it anew symmetrically. I did not cast it on the floor as you have done, with your so lamentable absence of order and method.'

'The King of Clubs'

‘My friend Hastings is, as you say in England, *all at the seaside.*’

‘The Jewel Robbery at the Grand Metropolitan’

'Do not enrage yourself, Hastings.
In verity, I observe that there are times
when you almost detest me! Alas,
I suffer the penalties of greatness.'

'The Million Dollar Bond Robbery'

'If you would only use the brains the good God has given you. Sometimes I really am tempted to believe that by inadvertence He passed you by.'

Lord Edgware Dies

'I did not deceive you, *mon ami*. At most, I permitted you to deceive yourself.'

The Mysterious Affair at Styles

'Is that a way to fold a coat...? You have no sense of proportion Hastings. We cannot catch a train earlier than the time that it leaves, and to ruin one's clothes will not be the least helpful in preventing a murder.'

The ABC Murders

‘If only, Hastings, you would part your hair in the middle instead of at the side! What a difference it would make to the symmetry of your appearance. And your moustache. If you must have a moustache, let it be a real moustache – a thing of beauty such as mine.’

Peril at End House

‘But for my quick eyes, the eyes of a cat, Hercule Poirot might now be crushed out of existence – a terrible calamity for the world. And you, too, *mon ami* – though that would not be such a national catastrophe.’

The Big Four

'Ah, *mon ami*, you know my little weakness! Always I have a desire to keep the threads in my own hands up to the last minute. But have no fear. I will reveal all when the time comes. I want no credit – the affair shall be yours, on the condition that you permit me to play out the *dénouement* my own way.'

'The Affair at the Victory Ball'

'Do you know, my friend, that each one of us is a dark mystery, a maze of conflicting passions and desire and attitudes? *Mais oui, c'est vrai*. One makes one's little judgements – but nine times out of ten one is wrong... Even Hercule Poirot!'

Lord Edgware Dies

'The good inspector believes in matter in motion. He travels; he measures footprints; he collects mud and cigarette-ash! He is extremely busy! He is zealous beyond words! And if I mentioned psychology to him, do you know what he would do, my friend? He would smile! He would say to himself: "Poor old Poirot! He ages! He grows senile!" Japp is the "younger generation knocking on the door". And *ma foi!* They are so busy knocking that they do not notice that the door is open!'

'The Plymouth Express'

POSTSCRIPT

THE LAST WORD

by Agatha Christie

'In the course of an excavation, when something comes up out of the ground, everything is cleared away very carefully all around it. You take away the loose earth, and you scrape here and there with a knife until finally your object is there, all alone, ready to be drawn and photographed with no extraneous matter confusing it. That is what I have been seeking to do - clear away the extraneous matter so that we can see the truth - the naked shining truth.'

Death on the Nile

Poirot definitely has his favourite cases. In *The Murder of Roger Ackroyd* he was at his best investigating a crime in a quiet country village and using his knowledge of human nature to get at the truth. In *The Mystery of the Blue Train* I have always suspected he was not at his best, but the solving of *Lord Edgware Dies* was, I consider, a good piece of work on his part, though he gives some of the credit to Hastings.

Three Act Tragedy he regards as one of his failures, though most people do not agree with him. His final remark at the end of the case has amused many people. Remember how he said "It might have been me" when Mr Satterthwaite declared that anyone might have drunk the poisoned cocktail? Hercule Poirot cannot see why this should be thought so amusing - he considers that he merely stated an obvious truth.

Of all his cases, *Cards on the Table* was the murder which won his complete technical approval. The *Death on the Nile* saddened him, since he saw so much of the drama preceding the crime. And he undertook an *Appointment with Death* at the express desire of a man whose passion for the truth was equal with his own. The technical difficulties of the investigation also appealed to him, the necessity of reaching the truth in 24 hours without the help of expert evidence of any kind...

Well, I have given you some of my impressions of Hercule Poirot. They are based on an acquaintance of many years' standing. We are friends and partners. I am beholden to him financially.

On the other hand, he owes his very existence to me. In moments of irritation I point out that by a few strokes of the pen (or taps on the typewriter) I could destroy him utterly.

He replies grandiloquently: “Impossible to get rid of Hercule Poirot like that. He is much too clever!”

And so, as usual, the little man has the last word!

Agatha Christie

The article in this book was written by Agatha Christie to introduce the serialisation of her novel *Appointment With Death* in the *Daily Mail* in 1938.

‘You have a tendency, Hastings, to prefer the least likely. That, no doubt, is from reading too many detective stories.’

Peril at End House

REFERENCES

HERCULE POIROT: THE BOOKS

The Mysterious Affair at Styles
The Murder on the Links
Poirot Investigates
The Murder of Roger Ackroyd
The Big Four
The Mystery of the Blue Train
Peril at End House
Lord Edgware Dies
Murder on the Orient Express
Three Act Tragedy
Death in the Clouds
The ABC Murders
Murder in Mesopotamia
Cards on the Table
Murder in the Mews
Dumb Witness
Death on the Nile
Appointment With Death
Hercule Poirot's Christmas
Sad Cypress
One, Two, Buckle My Shoe
Evil Under the Sun
Five Little Pigs
The Hollow
The Labours of Hercules
Taken at the Flood
Mrs McGinty's Dead
After the Funeral
Hickory Dickory Dock
Dead Man's Folly
Cat Among the Pigeons
The Adventure of the Christmas Pudding
The Clocks
Third Girl
Hallowe'en Party
Elephants Can Remember
Poirot's Early Cases
Curtain: Poirot's Last Case

HERCULE POIROT: THE SHORT STORIES

Poirot Investigates

'The Jewel Robbery at the Grand Metropolitan'
'The Disappearance of Mr Davenheim'
'The Adventure of the "Western Star"'
'The Tragedy of Marsdon Manor'
'The Kidnapped Prime Minister'
'The Million Dollar Bond Robbery'
'The Adventure of the Cheap Flat'
'The Mystery of Hunter's Lodge'
'The Adventure of the Egyptian Tomb'
'The Adventure of the Italian Nobleman'
'The Case of the Missing Will'

Poirot's Early Cases

'The Affair at the Victory Ball'
'The King of Clubs'
'The Plymouth Express'
'The Chocolate Box'
'The Veiled Lady'
'The Adventure of Johnny Waverley'
'The Market Basing Mystery'
'The Adventure of the Clapham Cook'
'The Lost Mine'
'The Cornish Mystery'
'The Double Clue'
'The Lemesurier Inheritance'
'Double Sin'
'Wasps' Nest'
'The Third-Floor Flat'
'How Does Your Garden Grow?'
'Problem at Sea'
'The Submarine Plans'

Murder in the Mews
'The Incredible Theft'
'Dead Man's Mirror'
'Triangle at Rhodes'
'Murder in the Mews'

The Adventure of the Christmas Pudding
'The Adventure of the Christmas Pudding'
'The Under Dog'
'The Mystery of the Spanish Chest'
'The Dream'
'Four-and-Twenty Blackbirds'

Problem at Pollensa Bay
'Yellow Iris'
'The Second Gong'

The Labours of Hercules
'The Nemean Lion'
'The Lernean Hydra'
'The Arcadian Deer'
'The Erymanthian Boar'
'The Augean Stables'
'The Stymphalean Birds'
'The Cretan Bull'
'The Horses of Diomedes'
'The Girdle of Hyppolita'
'The Flock of Geryon'
'The Apples of the Hesperides'
'The Capture of Cerberus'

While the Light Lasts
'Christmas Adventure'
'The Mystery of the Baghdad Chest'

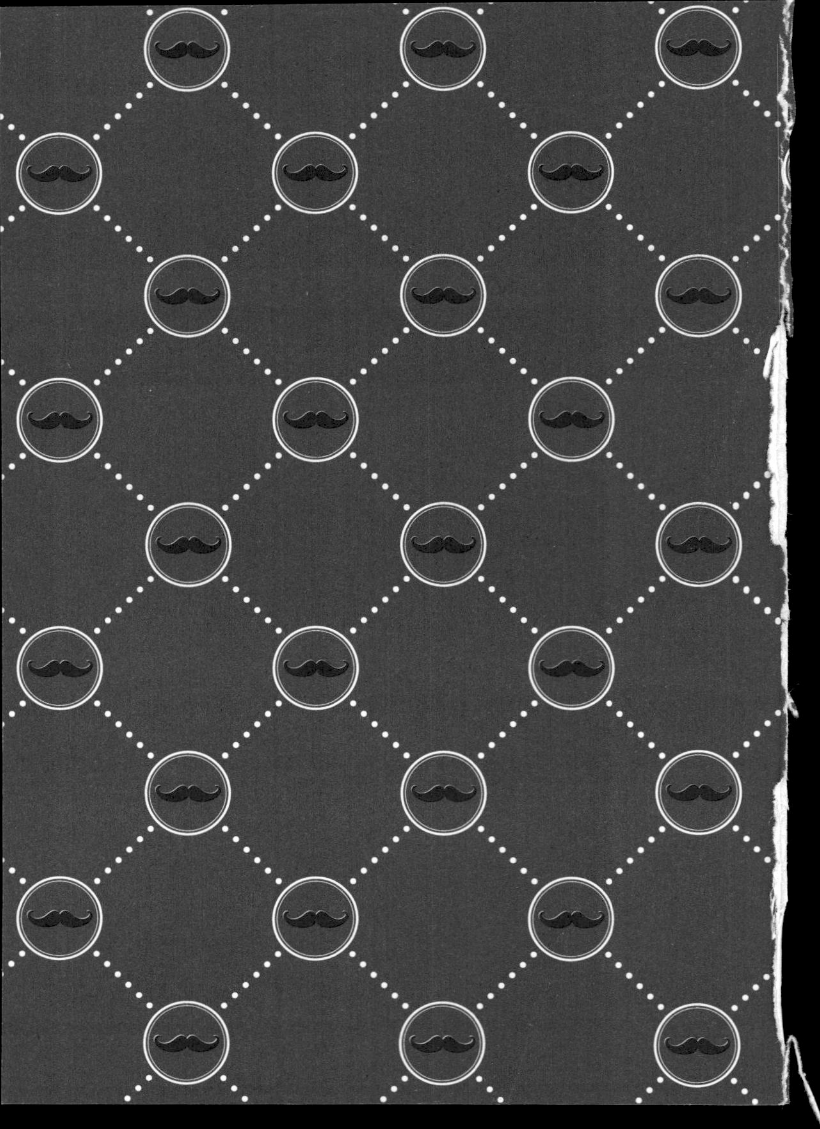